This book belongs to:

_____

A catalogue record for this book is available from the British Library

Published by Ladybird Books Ltd
80 Strand, London, WC2R ORL
A Penguin Company

4 6 8 10 9 7 5
© LADYBIRD BOOKS LTD MMVIII
LADYBIRD and the device of a Ladybird are trademarks of Ladybird Books Ltd

ISBN: 978-1-84646-868-1

Printed in China

Stories for

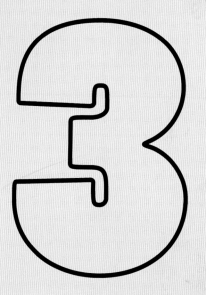

3

year olds

Written by Joan Stimson
Illustrated by Ingela Peterson

No room for Panda

Lucy's dad was a sailor. He sailed the world in a big ship. When he came home, he liked to bring presents.

One day Lucy's dad sailed to China.

When he came home, he brought a very special present. In fact you could say it was a giant present. Lucy's dad had brought home a panda.

Lucy was thrilled. Her mum was shocked. She didn't know if they had room for a panda.

That night Panda slept in Lucy's bed. It was a bit of a squash.

The next day Lucy got ready for playgroup. She waited at the bus stop with Mum and Panda.

Panda stuck his paw out when the bus came. But the bus conductor was firm. "Sorry," he said. "Panda's too big for my bus."

Mum, Lucy and Panda walked all the way to playgroup.

Panda shook hands with Miss Roberts. He was keen to join in.

But Panda got stuck – halfway down the playgroup slide.

Miss Roberts called the fire brigade. Then she called Lucy's mum.
"I'm sorry," she said. "Panda's too wide for playgroup."

Mum collected Lucy and Panda early.
She decided to do some shopping.

Panda had never been to a supermarket.
He wanted to ride in the trolley. But
Panda was too heavy. He squashed the
trolley flat.

"I'm sorry," said
the manager. "Panda
will have to shop
somewhere else."

Lucy trudged home with Mum and Panda. They told Dad all about it.

Lucy's dad had a brainwave. "Let's go swimming," he said. "There will be plenty of room for Panda."

The swimming trip began well. Panda could swim like a fish. He gave the children rides on his back.

But Panda was too frisky. He made great waves in the pool.

The attendant blew his whistle. "Time's up, Panda," he said. "I'm getting soaked!"

Lucy's mum helped to dry Panda.

Mum, Dad, Lucy and Panda started to walk home. On their way they passed the zoo. Panda tugged at Lucy's hand. He wanted to see the other animals.

The zookeeper smiled at Panda. "No charge for pandas!" he said.

Suddenly everyone knew what to do.
Mum, Dad and Lucy agreed to leave
Panda at the zoo. The keeper said they
could visit whenever they wanted.

Panda looked round his new home. He
liked the company. He liked the space.

Mum, Dad and Lucy waved goodbye to
Panda. Then they went home – on
the bus!

Nigel's toothache

Ben had a pet crocodile. The crocodile was called Nigel. Nigel was a very well behaved pet.

He kept his room clean. He wiped his feet. He ate up all his meals, especially when there was cherry pie.

One day Nigel didn't feel well. He left his egg at breakfast. He didn't want to play. Nigel had toothache.

Ben's mum rang the dentist. Nigel went upstairs to clean his teeth. He jumped into the bath and turned on the tap. He scrubbed his teeth with a body brush. It was just the right size for Nigel.

Ben, Mum and Nigel set off for the dentist.

"Sit down, Nigel," said Mr Webb kindly. He tucked a napkin under Nigel's chin. "Now, what seems to be the trouble?"

Nigel shook his head sadly.

The nurse passed a small mirror to
Mr Webb.

"Open wide, Nigel," said Mr Webb.
Nigel did as he was told.

Mr Webb jumped back in alarm. He'd
never seen inside such a big mouth
before. He'd never seen so many teeth.

"Thank you, Nigel," said Mr Webb.
"You can close your mouth now."

Mr Webb looked at his little mirror.
He looked at his little instruments. He
looked down at Nigel and scratched
his head...

Then he had an idea.

He sent the nurse out to his car.
He asked her to fetch his tool kit.

"These look more like Nigel's size,"
he said. He laid out all his tools. Then
he said, "Open wide, Nigel." He knew
what to expect this time.

Mr Webb shone his big garage torch into Nigel's mouth. "Mmmm," he said. "What lovely clean teeth!"

"Aaah," said Nigel. Mr Webb prodded Nigel's back teeth gently with a screwdriver.

"Aaah," said Nigel. Mr Webb tapped Nigel's front teeth gently with a hammer.

"Aaah," said Nigel.

"Now I can see the trouble," said Mr Webb. He reached for his pliers and pulled a big cherry stone from between Nigel's teeth.

"Aaah! Oooh! Mmmm!" said Nigel. That was much more comfortable. The nurse gave Nigel a pink drink.

"Rinse, please, Nigel," said Mr Webb.

Ben, Mum and Nigel set off for home.

Nigel was beginning to feel hungry.
They all went into the supermarket.
Nigel pointed to one of the shelves.

There were rows of tins. Next to them was a big notice that said: *NEW IN! Cherry pie filling...with no stones!*

Indoor sports

It was freezing cold in the sea.
Mrs Penguin was worried.

Clive had a cough. Brenda had a
sore throat.

"No swimming today," said
Mrs Penguin firmly.

The penguins burst into tears. Clive had just learnt to float on his back. Brenda had a new beach ball. "We don't want to stay indoors," they wailed.

"And I don't want you under my feet," thought Mrs Penguin. Then she had an idea. "There's plenty of hot water," she said. "You can play in the bath."

Clive lay on his back and flapped his wings. Brenda dived for the soap. Then she fetched her ball.

Clive and Brenda had a competition to see who could make the biggest waves. The morning passed quickly.

"Lunch time," called Mrs Penguin.

The children rushed down in dressing gowns.

"Have you emptied the bath?" asked Mrs Penguin.

"Yes, Mum," said Clive.

"Yes, Mum," said Brenda. "And we didn't even pull out the plug!"

29